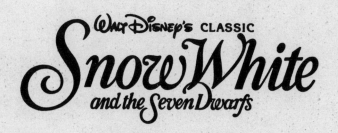

WALT DISNEY'S CLASSIC

Snow White

and the Seven Dwarfs

Based on Walt Disney's
full-length animated classic.

Adapted by Suzanne Weyn

SCHOLASTIC INC.
New York Toronto London Auckland Sydney

ISBN 0-590-41170-5

Published by Scholastic Inc.

12 11 10 9 8 7 6 5 4 3 2 1   7 8 9/8 0 1 2/9

Printed in the U.S.A.   11

First Scholastic printing, July 1987

Snow White
and the Seven Dwarfs

1

Once upon a time, there lived a lovely little princess named Snow White. She lived in a grand castle, but her life was not carefree. Her kind-hearted father was dead, and she was left in the care of her wicked stepmother, the Queen.

The vain Queen feared that someday Snow White's beauty would surpass her own. So she dressed the little princess in rags and forced her to work in the palace as a maid. She hoped that this hard life would keep Snow White's beauty from shining through.

Each day the Queen climbed the winding stone steps that led to a secret chamber at the very top of the castle. In the chamber stood a Magic Mirror. When the Queen entered the room she walked up to the Mirror and gazed into it, admiring her own great beauty. Then she raised her arms high over her head and shouted: "Slave in the Mirror, come from farthest space. Through wind and darkness I summon thee. Speak!"

The image of flames crackled in the Mirror, and

soon a horrible face appeared. "What wouldst thou know, my Queen?" it asked.

"Magic Mirror on the wall, who is the fairest one of all?" the Queen asked. Each time she asked this question the Queen was well pleased by the answer.

"You are the fairest in the land," the face in the Mirror answered.

So the days passed at the palace and Snow White grew ever lovelier, despite her hard life. And as time passed, the Queen's beauty began to fade, until one day when she talked to her Mirror, something unexpected happened. The Queen summoned the face in the mirror, but when she asked it who was fairest in the land, it did not answer her. "Speak! I command thee!" shrieked the Queen.

"Famed is thy beauty," said the Mirror, "but, hold, a lovely maid I see — rags cannot hide her gentle grace — alas, she is more fair than thee."

The Queen turned scarlet with rage. "Alas for her!" she cried. "Reveal her name, Mirror."

"Lips red as rose," the Mirror told her, "hair black as ebony, skin white as snow. . . ."

The Mirror did not have to tell the Queen any more. She already knew what it was about to say. "Snow White!" she growled.

Down in the courtyard Snow White was drawing water from the well. As far as she knew, this was a lovely spring day, the same as any other. Little did she dream that in the castle tower above her, the Queen was plotting a terrible scheme.

Snow White was dreaming of other things on this fine day. She was longing for a handsome prince who might someday come along and love her with all his heart.

As Snow White pulled up the heavy bucket, she smiled at the fat little pigeons who hopped around the stone well rim. "Shall I tell you a secret?" she asked them playfully. "This is a magic wishing well. If you make a wish and hear an echo in the well, then the wish will come true."

Snow White didn't really believe that the old castle well had this power, but just for fun, she leaned forward and told the well her dearest wish. She wished that her own true love would find her that very day.

"Today . . . today . . . today," the well echoed back.

"Oh!" cried Snow White softly, just a bit surprised to really hear the echo. "Wouldn't it be wonderful if my prince really did come to find me today?" The thought of seeing her prince made Snow White feel so lighthearted that she twirled around the courtyard, singing a little song.

The birds chirped along with Snow White as she danced and sang. They were not the only ones who heard her sweet song. A handsome prince happened to be riding alongside the courtyard wall. When the loveliness of Snow White's voice floated over the wall to him, he liked it so well that he just had to see who was singing. He got off his horse and climbed the courtyard wall. Snow White did not notice him as he watched her spin so prettily, but when he saw her, the Prince's heart filled with love.

Snow White danced back to the well. She leaned down to sing into the well one more time, but she jumped back in surprise when she saw the prince reflected in the well water.

"Hello," said the prince. "Did I frighten you?"

Snow White suddenly felt very shy. She hadn't really expected her prince to show up so soon. Confused, she turned and fled into the castle.

Once inside the castle, Snow White longed for another look at the handsome prince. She hurried to the balcony window and was glad to see him still in the courtyard.

The prince saw Snow White watching him from behind the velvet curtain and immediately began to sing her a love song that came straight from his heart.

Snow White forgot her shyness and stepped out onto the balcony so she could hear his wonderful words of love. She gazed at him and thought he was even more handsome than she'd imagined possible.

As Snow White looked lovingly at the prince,

other eyes watched him, as well. The wicked Queen watched from her high tower. "Curses," she hissed. "If that prince marries Snow White he will take her away and there will be nothing I can do. I must act today!"

2

The wicked Queen drummed her blood-red fingernails against the arms of her golden throne. "Come closer," she commanded the royal huntsman who stood before her.

"I have a job for you," she said. "Take Snow White far into the forest — find some secluded glen where she can pick wild flowers."

"Yes, your majesty," the huntsman answered, relieved that this was all the Queen wanted of him.

"And there," the Queen continued, "you will kill her!"

The huntsman stepped back in horror. "But, your majesty, the little princess!" he cried.

"Silence!" screamed the Queen. "You know the penalty if you fail."

The huntsman bowed his head. He did indeed know that death was the price he would pay if he failed to carry out the Queen's orders.

The Queen picked up a wooden box from the table beside her throne. She held it out to the huntsman.

"To make doubly sure you do not fail," she sneered, "bring Snow White's heart back to me in this box."

The box shook in the huntsman's trembling hands as he took it from the Queen. He bowed and fled from the royal chamber, trying not to think about the crime he was about to commit.

The huntsman found Snow White sweeping the kitchen floor and thinking about her prince. "The Queen wishes you to gather flowers for the palace," he told her. "I will take you into the forest glen to pick them."

"What fun," Snow White answered happily.

All the way through the forest, Snow White hummed the love song the prince had sung to her. She promised herself that the next time she saw the prince, she would overcome her shyness and speak to him.

The forest opened into a small field filled with purple and yellow wild flowers. "Aren't they pretty!" exclaimed Snow White. She set about at once gathering them. She stopped only long enough to comfort a baby bird who was hopping about looking for his parents.

Snow White didn't see the huntsman creep up slowly behind her. Nor did she see him pull his hunting knife slowly from its sheath. She was too busy tending the little bird. "Your Mamma and Poppa can't be far," she cooed to the frightened bird. "There they are."

As the little bird fluttered off to rejoin his parents, Snow White suddenly sensed the huntsman standing behind her. She whirled around in time to see his knife held high over her head, ready to strike.

Snow White screamed in terror. She stepped back, too frightened to run. The huntsman raised his hand higher, he stepped closer, and then. . . .

Then, slowly, he began to tremble. His knife fell to the ground as the huntsman dropped to his knees and buried his head in his hands. "I can't," he sobbed. "I can't do it — forgive me — I beg your highness to forgive me."

Snow White's heart pounded with fear, but she took pity on the miserable huntsman.

"Why?" she asked softly. "I don't understand."

"She's mad — jealous of you," the huntsman cried. "She'll stop at nothing!"

Snow White was still confused. "But who?" she asked.

"The Queen," said the huntsman.

"The Queen!" Snow White gasped in disbelief.

"Now, quickly, child," ordered the huntsman urgently, "Run! Run away and hide!"

"But . . . but," Snow White stammered, "where shall I go?"

"In the woods, anywhere," the huntsman shouted. He knew the Queen must never learn Snow White was alive — or she would kill both of them. "Now go, go," he cried. "Run! Hide!"

Snow White saw the terror in the huntsman's eyes, and she knew he meant what he said. Overcome with fear, Snow White raced off into the woods. She ran and ran until her lungs felt as if they would burst — and still she kept going.

She ran deeper and deeper into the forest to where the trees grew taller and closer together. The setting sun cast eerie shadows around the forest. Soon night fell, spreading a blanket of darkness over everything.

Snow White stumbled. She felt leathery bat wings sweep by her cheek. Horrible faces loomed up out of the darkness at her. Fingers reached out and clutched her skirt.

Snow White screamed and ran blindly through the forest. Splash! She slipped into a shallow stream. There was something in the water with her. It had piercing yellow eyes. Surely it must be an alligator!

Snow White pulled herself out of the stream and looked around. The forest was filled with shrill sounds. All around her thousands of eyes stared.

"I have run into a forest of monsters," Snow White said to herself. "And I will never, ever get out of here alive!" Overcome with grief and terror, Snow White collapsed to the ground.

3

The dawn's pink and golden light found Snow White still lying on the cold ground surrounded by the creatures who had so terrified her in the darkness — but these creatures were not monsters at all. Looking down at Snow White were deer, squirrels, chipmunks, birds, and all sorts of woodland creatures. She'd been so frightened of the forest that Snow White had imagined them to be monsters.

The animals were very curious about Snow White — for this was a part of the forest few people ever visited. One little bunny hopped up to Snow White and sniffed. This awakened the weary princess who lifted her head and was startled to find herself eye to eye with a rabbit.

"Oh!" she cried in surprise, sending the animals scurrying for cover. "Please don't run away," she called after them. "I won't hurt you."

One by one the animals stuck their heads out from their hiding places and studied Snow White from afar. She seemed gentle — but the animals weren't sure if they should trust her.

"I'm awfully sorry. I didn't mean to frighten you," Snow White apologized, rubbing the sleep from her eyes. "But you don't know what I've been through."

Snow White knew now that she had nothing to fear from the creatures of the forest. She suddenly felt foolish for having been so frightened. "I'm so ashamed of the fuss I made," she told the animals, who were moving ever closer to her. "And all because I was so afraid."

Suddenly Snow White remembered everything that had happened the day before — the Queen's evil plan, the huntsman's knife — and she trembled. But Snow White promised herself never to let fear overcome her again, no matter what the future held.

"What do *you* do when things go wrong?" she asked the birds who sat in the branches above her.

"Chirp! Chirp! Chirp!" they sang merrily.

"Of course," Snow White said with a smile, "you sing a song."

The birds chirped again and sang happily. Snow White felt better right away. She joined their song. "Ah — ah-ah-ah," she sang in her high, lovely voice.

The more Snow White sang, the better she felt. Soon her song had chased all her cares away. Snow White felt wonderful!

"I'm really quite happy now," she told the little

group of animals. "I'm sure I'll get along somehow. Everything is going to be all right." A deer nuzzled its nose into Snow White's hand to assure her that everything would be just fine.

"But I do need a place to sleep at night," Snow White said. "I can't sleep in the ground like you rabbits. Or in a tree as you squirrels do. And I'm sure no nest could possibly be big enough for me." The birds twittered with laughter at the thought of Snow White sitting in a nest.

"Do any of you know a place where I can stay?" she asked. The birds above Snow White chirped a "Yes."

"Is it somewhere in the woods?" she asked.

The deer nodded, "Yes."

"Will you take me there?" Snow White asked. Three birds flew down and took hold of Snow White's cape. They pulled her along as they flew through the forest. The other animals followed.

"Where could they be taking me," Snow White wondered. Was it to a cave? Or did they know of a soft, dried-up riverbed? Snow White tried to guess, but she could never in a million years have imagined the place the animals had in mind.

Snow White and the animals walked through the woods until they came to a spot where the forest was met by an open, sloping glen. Snow White parted the branches and looked into the clearing.

Snow White wondered if she was dreaming. She

rubbed her eyes and looked again. "Oh, it's adorable!" she cried happily. There, in the glen, on the far side of a small bridge stood a small cottage with a straw roof and a stone chimney.

"It's just like a doll's house!" exclaimed Snow White as she ran over the little footbridge toward the cottage.

Her animal friends caught up to Snow White at the front of the cottage. Snow White looked around. There was no one around the cottage. She walked up to the front window. It was black with grimy dirt. She wiped a circle in the dirt and peered in. "Oooooh! It's dark inside," she told the animals.

Snow White knocked on the front door. There was no answer. "Guess there's no one home," she said. She jiggled the doorknob and discovered that the door was unlocked. She pushed it open. "Hello," she called. "May I come in?" There was still no response.

Slowly, Snow White stepped into the dark cottage and looked around. "Oh my, my, my," she muttered. This was not what she had expected to find at all.

4

W hat an awful mess!" said Snow White. "Who could possibly live here?"

She stepped forward and bumped into a tiny chair that sent up a cloud of dust. Snow White wiped the chair with her hand and sat down lightly on it. "What a cute little chair," she said. She looked around and saw six more dirty little chairs exactly like it. When Snow White saw how small the chairs were, she had a thought. "Must be seven very untidy little children who live here," she said.

Snow White had never seen such a dirty place in her life! The table in the middle of the room was piled high with dirty dishes. A tiny pickax lay on the floor. When she lifted the lid of an old pot on the stove she found a tiny shoe inside!

"And just look at this fireplace," she said to the animals as she blew a layer of dust from it. "There are cobwebs everywhere."

Snow White noticed a broom standing in the corner of the room. She picked it up and looked at the

unbroken bristles. "Why, they've never swept this room," she said in disbelief. "You'd think their mother would. . . ."

A sad thought suddenly occurred to Snow White. "Maybe they have no mother."

The doe and her fawn shook their heads sadly in agreement. "They're orphans," sighed kind-hearted Snow White. "That's too bad." Snow White's heart went out to the poor messy children with no one to look after them.

"I know," she said, "we'll clean the house and surprise them. Then maybe they'll let me stay."

Snow White took off her cape and got right to work. "I'll use the broom," she said to the animals, "while you wash the dishes and tidy the room."

The animals were glad to help. The turtles carried stacks of dishes to the sink. The squirrels knocked down cobwebs with their tails. The birds flew to and fro putting things in order.

As the birds worked they sang a cheery tune. Snow White recognized their song right away and joined them.

The animals were not experienced house-keepers. Snow White had to stop the fawn from licking the dishes clean. And the chipmunk brothers had to be told not to sweep the dirt under the rug. But Snow White knew they were doing their best, and before long the little cottage was shiny and clean.

Snow White then looked in the cupboards for food. She found everything she needed to make a kettle of vegetable soup and an apple pie. She set the soup to simmer over the fireplace, and when the apple pie was prepared, she put it out to cool on the windowsill.

"Now let's see what's upstairs," Snow White suggested. She lit a candle and held it up to light the way as she climbed the wooden steps to the second floor. Timidly, the animals followed her up the stairs.

At the top of the stairs stood a small door. Snow White pushed it open, and she stepped into a low, narrow room. "What adorable little beds," she remarked to the animals who had followed her into the room. There against the walls were seven little beds with thick wooden frames.

"And look, they have their names carved on them," she said, pointing to the carvings on each footboard. One by one, Snow White read the names out loud to the animals. "Doc, Happy, Sneezy, Dopey . . . what funny names for children," she said with a laugh. "Grumpy, Bashful, and Sleepy," she continued.

As she read the last name, Snow White yawned and stretched. "I'm a little sleepy myself," she said. The animals agreed. All that housework had worn them out. Soon they were yawning along with Snow White.

Snow White stretched out across three of the tiny beds. The birds covered her with a sheet, put out her candle, and settled in on the bedposts. The other animals curled up for naps all around the room.

The last of the animals was about to nod off, when the mother doe pricked up her ears. She'd heard a sound coming through the forest. It was a sound she had heard before. The squirrels were the next to hear it. Soon all the animals were awake. They stood alert and listening.

The sound was getting nearer and nearer the cottage. The animals panicked and raced down the stairs — leaving Snow White sound asleep and alone in the strange cottage.

5

If Snow White had known who really lived in the cottage, she might not have slept so easily. It wasn't owned by seven messy children at all. It belonged to seven little men — the Seven Dwarfs.

The dwarfs worked in a magical jewel mine not far from their cottage. Each day they pulled a fortune in jewels from the mine. The dwarfs loved their hard work so much that they sang as they chipped away at the walls of the mine.

On this day, like every other, the dwarfs stopped working when the sun began to set. They gathered their jewels together in a pile and headed for home. The dwarfs always walked in a line with Doc holding a lantern in the lead and the dwarf named Dopey holding another lantern at the end of the line. As they trudged through the darkening forest, they sang their "Going Home Song" at the tops of their lungs.

This song was what the animals had heard coming toward the cottage. They knew that it meant the dwarfs would soon come home and discover the changes in their cottage.

The dwarfs knew something unusual was going on in their cottage as soon as they saw it.

"Look! Our house," cried kindly old Doc. "The lit's light . . . I mean, the light's lit."

The dwarfs were on the alert for danger. They crept cautiously up to the house, sneaking from tree to tree.

"Door's open," Doc whispered. "Chimney's smokin' — somethin's in there."

"Maybe a ghost," said Happy, with a shiver.

"Or a goblin," added Bashful.

"Or a dragon," suggested Sneezy.

Happy had an idea. "Let's sneak up on whatever's inside," he said.

"Good idea!" agreed Doc. "We'll squeak up — uh, I mean, sneak up. Come on hen — I mean, men — follow me!"

Crouching low, the dwarfs tiptoed to the front of the cottage. They peered into the window, and, seeing no one inside, they quietly entered through the front door.

"Careful men," warned Doc in a whisper. "Search every cook 'n' nanny — I mean hook 'n' granny, uh, crooked fan — I mean, search everywhere!"

The group separated and began to explore. They soon realized that things were very different in their cottage from the way they'd left them.

"Look!" whispered Doc excitedly, "The floor. It's been swept!"

Grumpy rubbed his fingers across his little chair. There wasn't a speck of dirt on it! "Chair's been dusted," he grumbled.

"Our window's been washed," added Happy.

"Gosh. Our cobwebs is missin'," said Bashful, gazing up at the ceiling.

"Why . . . why . . . why, the whole place is clean!" said Doc, amazed.

"There's dirty work afoot!" said Grumpy. He didn't like this one bit. He wanted his old dirty cottage back the way it was!

The dwarfs continued to look around. "Hey, someone stole our dishes," cried Sneezy, looking into the empty sink.

"They ain't stole," Happy told him. "They're here, hid in the cupboard."

"All our sugar is gone," Bashful told the rest. As he spoke they noticed the pie sitting on the windowsill and smelled the delicious aroma rising up from the fireplace.

Bashful lifted the lid of the heavy iron kettle. "Somethin's cookin'."

"Smells good," Happy said, grabbing a clean spoon from the cupboard and running toward the kettle.

"Don't touch it, you fools!" cried Grumpy. "It

might be poison." Just as he said the word "poison," the kettle let off a burst of steam. "See," said Grumpy. "It's witches' brew."

Doc's eyes traveled around the neat room. He wasn't quite sure, but maybe — just maybe — he liked the room this way. His eyes stopped at a strange sight. "Look what's happened to our stable — uh, I mean table," he said.

Bashful grabbed the yellow flowers that stood in a vase on the cleaned-off table. "Flowers," he said, giving them a sniff. He showed them to Sneezy, who had come up behind him. "Look — goldenrod," he said to Sneezy, offering Sneezy the flowers to smell.

This was a mistake, because Sneezy had terrible hayfever and goldenrod always made him sneeze. "Take it away!" said Sneezy, holding his hand up. "You know I can't stand it. I cah — I cas — Achooooooooooooo!"

Sneezy sneezed so hard that the dwarfs went flying against the wall. They smashed into one another, making a terrible racket.

"Ya crazy fool!" scolded Grumpy in a loud whisper. "A fine time to pick to sneeze. Do you wanna get us all killed?"

All this time the forest animals were slowly creeping back toward the cottage. They were amused to see the dwarfs in such an uproar. Two little birds flew in the door and perched on the ceiling rafter. Just to tease the dwarfs, they pecked on the wooden beam.

"Wha — what — what was that?" asked Happy fearfully.

"That's IT!" said Doc.

"Sounded close," Bashful added.

"It's in this very room — right now," Grumpy told them knowingly.

The birds twittered with laughter. Then, just for the fun of it, they let out an awful shriek that sent the frightened dwarfs running in all directions, looking for places to hide. Sneezy dove into a large jar. Sleepy hid in a bucket. Dopey leaped into the woodpile, and Happy ran behind a chair. Bashful ducked under the stairs, and Grumpy crawled into a potato sack.

When no monster appeared, Doc was the first to speak. "It's up there," he said, pointing to the top of the stairs.

"Yeah. In the bedroom," Bashful added.

The dwarfs agreed that someone would have to go up and see who — or what — was up there. Little Dopey was always chosen for the unpleasant jobs because he didn't speak — and so he wouldn't say "no." This time was the same. Dopey backed away when he saw all the dwarfs staring at him. He tried to run for the door, but the dwarfs dragged him back to the stairs.

With quivering hands, Doc gave Dopey a candle to light the way up the dark stairs. "Now don't be nervous," he told Dopey.

The dwarfs had to give poor Dopey a shove to get him started up the stairs. Shaking with fear, Dopey climbed the steps. When he got to the middle, he felt too frightened to go on. He turned and faced the dwarfs who stood at the bottom of the stairs.

"Don't be afraid," whispered Doc. All the dwarfs urged Dopey on. "We're right behind you!"

With a gulp of fear, Dopey continued his lonely climb. When he reached the top, Dopey quickly pushed open the bedroom door and stuck his candle into the dark room. He shut his eyes tightly, expecting to hear the roar of a monster.

There was no sound coming from the bedroom, so Dopey tiptoed in, holding his candle high. He looked all around. There didn't seem to be anyone there.

Then, suddenly, Snow White stirred in her sleep. Buried under the white sheets of the bedding, she yawned and stretched.

Dopey leaped into the air in fright. He raced out of the room and tumbled pell-mell down the steps.

"Here it comes!" cried Sneezy at the bottom of the stairs. "It's chasing Dopey."

"Run fer yer lives!" cried Grumpy, making a dash for the front door. The other dwarfs were quickly behind him. They raced out the front door and slammed it shut, not realizing they had locked Dopey inside.

Dopey bumped up against the shut door. He was frantic to escape from the horrible monster he'd seen in the bed. He banged on the door with all his might.

The more Dopey banged and tugged on the door, the more the dwarfs leaned their weight against it on the other side. They thought Dopey was the monster trying to get out of the house. "It's after us!" they shouted. "Don't let it out. Hold it shut!"

Desperate to get out, Dopey yanked on the door handle so hard that it came flying off and sent Dopey sailing backwards into the cupboards. The racket of clattering pots and pans that tumbled onto Dopey's head from the cupboard terrified the dwarfs outside. They ran from the door and hid behind the nearby trees.

Seeing that the door had now swung open, Dopey made a dash out of the house. Blinded by fear, the dwarfs mistook him for the monster and wasted no time in pouncing on him, pounding him with their tough little fists. "Give it to him!" they shouted. "Don't let him get away. Take that . . . and that . . . and — "

"Hold on there!" cried Doc. "It's only — only Dopey."

The dwarfs pulled their little friend to his feet

and dusted him off. They were full of questions, which they asked him all at once.

"Did you see it?"

"How big was it?"

"Has it got horns?"

"Was it a dragon?"

Dopey acted out his answer with gestures and faces. "He says it's a monster a-a-asleep in our beds," said Doc.

"Let's attack," said Grumpy, "while it's still sleepin'."

The group thought this was a good idea. Doc took the lead as they marched bravely back to the cottage. They grabbed their pickaxes at the front door, and together they climbed the stairs. Cautiously they crept into the bedroom, their axes ready to strike.

"Hmmmmm," Snow White sighed in her sleep. The dwarfs jumped back, frightened. They regained their courage and moved closer to the beds. There they saw Snow White still asleep, buried under the sheets.

"What a monster!" they whispered. "Covers three beds. Let's kill it before it wakes up!"

"Which end do we kill?" Bashful wanted to know, but no one could give him an answer.

Doc had a plan. "We'll clobber it, when — when I count to three," he instructed them. "Get your weapons ready. One . . . two . . . three!"

31

6

Just as the dwarfs were about to strike what they thought was a sleeping monster, Doc pulled the sheet away from their foe. He froze in shock at the sight before him.

"Why — i — i — it's a girl!" he gasped.

"She's a might purty," said Sneezy, putting down his pickax beside him.

"She's beautiful — just like an angel," Bashful agreed.

Grumpy wasn't as quick to be won over by this sleeping stranger. "Angel, huh," he grumbled. "She's a female, an' all females is poison. They're fulla wicked wiles."

"What are wicked wiles?" asked Bashful.

"I don't know," Grumpy admitted, "but I'm agin' 'em."

"Shhh," said Doc, "not so loud. You'll wake her up."

"Aw — let her wake up," replied Grumpy sourly. "She don't belong here nohow."

Snow White stretched in her sleep. She rolled to the side.

"Look out. She's movin'!" cried Bashful.

"She's wakin' up!" yelled Happy with alarm.

The dwarfs looked at Doc. "What'll we do?" they asked.

"Hide!" shouted Doc, seeing that Snow White was about to open her eyes. The dwarfs thought this was good advice. They quickly ducked down below the foot of the bed.

Snow White rubbed the sleep from her eyes and sat up in bed. She was sure she'd heard a noise.

"Oh, dear," she said to herself, "I wonder if the children are . . ." She never finished her thought because suddenly seven little faces popped up to look at her from the foot of the bed.

"Aaaahhh!" Snow White screamed, pulling the covers over herself for protection. She'd never seen anything like these Seven Dwarfs before!

Snow White's scream frightened the dwarfs who ducked down again. Then, summoning their courage, they peeked back up at her one by one.

"Oh! Why, you're little men," said Snow White, seeing now that they were not really so frightening. "How do you do?"

The dwarfs had never heard this polite phrase before, and it puzzled them. They stared at one another and then back at Snow White.

"I said, 'How do you do?' " Snow White repeated.

"How do you do what?" snapped Grumpy.

Snow White smiled at him. "You can talk! I'm so glad. Now don't tell me who you are. Let me guess."

She looked over the little men in their brightly colored coats. "You're Doc," she said to the kindly old dwarf whose glasses were slipping from his nose.

"Uh — huh — why — yeah — uh, eh, that's true," he replied, proud to be recognized.

Next Snow White looked at the dwarf who was gazing up at her shyly. "And you're — you're Bashful," she guessed correctly.

Bashful blushed a deep crimson red. "Oh, gosh! Heh — uh!" he stammered, tying his white beard into a knot.

Just then Sleepy looked at his little bed and yawned. "You're Sleepy," said Snow White with a laugh.

"How'd you guess?" asked Sleepy, not understanding how he had given himself away.

"And you — " said Snow White, looking at the dwarf with a red nose who was trying to stifle a sneeze. "You're Sneezy."

"Achooo!" sneezed Sneezy, causing Happy to fall on the floor, doubled over with laughter.

"And you must be — " said Snow White, watching the fat, jolly dwarf rolling on the floor, holding his sides.

"Happy — ma'am — that's me," he told her, eager to make her job easy. "And this is Dopey. He don't talk none." Little Dopey bowed and took off his cap in greeting.

"You mean he can't talk?" asked Snow White.

"He don't know. He never tried," Happy told her.

"Oh. That's too bad," Snow White said, pleasantly, smiling at Dopey. Then Snow White saw a pair of scowling eyes gazing at her sternly. She knew right away who this dwarf was. "You must be Grumpy."

Grumpy wouldn't even answer until Doc reminded him to be polite with a poke in the ribs. "Yeah," he mumbled, ignoring the laughter of the other dwarfs.

Feeling grouchy as ever, Grumpy turned to Doc and said, "We know who we are. Ask her who she is and what she's a-doin' here."

Doc took on a serious expression and stepped forward. "Humph," he cleared his throat. "What are you and who are you doin' — uh — uh — I mean, what are you — who are you, my dear?"

"Oh, how silly of me! I'm Snow White."

The dwarfs gasped. "Snow White! The princess?"

"Yes," she answered sweetly.

"Well, well, my — my — my dear princess," said Doc, very much impressed to find a princess in his little cottage. "We're, uh — we're honored. Yes, we're — ah — "

"Mad as hornets!" Grumpy chimed in.

"Mad as hornets," continued Doc, not realizing

what he was saying. "No, no — we're bad as cor-
nets — no, no — bad as — what was I sayin'?"

"Nothin'!" yelled Grumpy. "You was just standin'
there sputter'n' like a doodle bug."

The good-tempered Doc grew angry at Grumpy's
words. "Wh — wh — who's butter'n' like a spoodle
dug? Who's — wuh — huh — huh — gutter glove."

"Aw, shut up and tell her to git out!" griped
Grumpy.

Snow White went pale with fright at Grumpy's
words. "Please don't send me away," she pleaded.
"If you do, she'll kill me."

This alarmed the dwarfs who asked, all together,
"Kill you! Who will? Yes, who?"

"My stepmother, the Queen," Snow White told
them.

"The Queen!" cried the dwarfs at once. They had
all heard of the Queen's wicked ways.

"She's bad," said Happy, who usually thought
well of everyone.

"She's bighty bean," agreed Sneezy. Just thinking
of the Queen made him feel like sneezing.

"She's an old witch," declared Grumpy decidedly.
He didn't want anything to do with angering the
Queen. "I'm warnin' ya," he said, "if the Queen finds
her here, she'll sweep down and get all of us."

"But she doesn't know where I am," said Snow
White.

"She doesn't, eh," said Grumpy, wearing an

expression of disbelief. "She knows everything. She's fulla black magic. She can make herself invisible!"

Grumpy circled around the room dramatically. "She might be in this room." He stared menacingly at the other dwarfs. "In this very room RIGHT NOW!"

The dwarfs shivered at the meaning of Grumpy's words. Perhaps it wasn't wise to risk the Queen's anger.

"Oh, she'll never find me here," said Snow White. "And if you let me stay, I'll keep house for you. I'll wash and sew, sweep and cook."

"Cook!" cried the dwarfs.

"Uh — can you make dapple lumpkins — uh — lumple dapplins — "

"Apple dumplin's," said Grumpy and Sneezy, coming to Doc's aid.

"Ah — yes — crapple dumpkins," said Doc.

"Yes," answered Snow White, "and plum pudding and gooseberry pie."

"Ahhhhhh!" sighed the dwarfs. "Gooseberry pie." The dwarfs hadn't had gooseberry pie since — well, they couldn't even remember when.

"Hooray!" they shouted. "She stays!"

Snow White clapped her hands with pleasure, then she sniffed the air and remembered her soup cooking over the fire. She jumped out of bed and ran downstairs to make sure it wasn't burning.

The dwarfs smelled the soup, too. They scrambled down the stairs behind Snow White, yelling, "Ah! Soup! Hooray!"

Snow White stirred the kettle. The soup was just right. By now the aroma of the soup filled the room. The hungry dwarfs grabbed their bowls from the cupboard and crowded around the steaming pot.

Snow White turned and looked at their eager faces. "Ah, ah, ah," she said. "There's something you have to do before you eat."

When Snow White told the dwarfs what she wanted them to do, they were stunned. They staggered back in horror. This was really asking too much!

7

W ash!" cried the panic-stricken dwarfs. This was unheard of! Unbelievable!

"Heh, I knew there was a catch to it," grumbled Grumpy, folding his arms stubbornly.

"Why wash?" asked Bashful.

"What for? We ain't goin' nowhere," said Happy.

"T'ain't New Year's," Doc pointed out.

"Oh, perhaps you have washed already," Snow White said, stirring the kettle.

"Perhaps we — yes, er — perhaps we have," said Doc slyly, winking at the other dwarfs.

"But when?" Snow White asked, turning to look at him. He was so dirty she couldn't believe he had washed in a long time.

"When — er — you said when — " Doc looked at the others for help. "I — uh — last week — uh — month, uh, year — I — uh — recently."

That sounded good to the dwarfs. "Yes, recently," they agreed, nodding their heads.

Snow White was not so easily fooled. "Oh, re-

cently. Hmmmmm," she said. "Let me see your hands." The dwarfs quickly hid their hands behind their backs.

"Come on now, let me see your hands," Snow White coaxed gently.

Finally Doc stuck out his grubby, dirt-blackened hands. "Why, Doc, I'm surprised," Snow White scolded mildly. One by one each of the dwarfs held out his hands, and each pair was dirtier than the next. Snow White inspected them all, saying, "Oh, my, my, my. Shocking. Worse than I thought. Goodness me, this will never do."

The dwarfs hid their hands again and looked up at Snow White sheepishly. "March straight outside and wash, or you'll not get a bite to eat," she told them.

The smell of the soup floated through the room. The dwarfs couldn't bear not to get some of that delicious soup. Doc nodded to the others and began to march toward the door. Bashful, Sneezy, Sleepy, Happy, and Dopey followed him out. Only Grumpy stood still as a statue, his arms folded firmly across his chest.

"Aren't you going to wash?" Snow White asked him. Grumpy wouldn't answer her. He just stood there frowning. "What's the matter?" Snow White asked kindly. "Cat got your tongue?"

Grumpy suddenly whirled around and stuck out his tongue at Snow White. Then he turned his back on her and stomped off — crashing smack into the closed door.

Snow White smothered a giggle with her hand. "Aw, did you hurt yourself?" she asked, bending down to help the grouchy little fellow.

"Heh!" Grumpy snorted at her. He pulled his cap down over his eyes and marched out to join the others in the yard.

Outside the dwarfs were circling a tub of water nervously. "Courage, men, courage," Doc said. "Be brave."

Happy stuck the very tip of his finger into the tub. "Gosh, it's wet," he muttered.

Sneezy felt the water next. "Brrr! It's cold, too."

Bashful turned to Doc. "We ain't really gonna do it, are we?"

Doc thought for a minute. "Well — it — it'll please the princess."

"I'll take a chance for her," said Happy bravely.

"Me, too!" cried all the other dwarfs — except Grumpy.

"Huh! Her wiles are beginning to work," Grumpy warned. "Ya give 'em a inch and they'll walk all over ya."

"Uh — don't listen to that old — warthog," Doc told the others. "Come on now, men."

"How hard do ya scrub?" asked Sneezy.

"Will our whiskers shrink?" Sleepy wanted to know.

44

"Do ya get *in* the tub?" Happy asked.

"Do you have to wash where it doesn't show?" Bashful asked with dread in his voice.

"Everyone calm down," said Doc. "It's easy. Just watch me."

With that, Doc splashed the cold water onto his face and rubbed it all around. "Use the soap," Doc continued.

Happy and Bashful dipped their hands in the water and made a lather with the soap. Sneezy and Sleepy rubbed the soap on their faces.

Soon everyone but Grumpy was covered with soapy lather and splashing water all over. It wasn't nearly as terrible as they had expected.

In fact, the dwarfs were having lots of fun. All except Grumpy, who watched them with a disgusted expression on his face.

"Bunch of old nanny goats," he grumbled. "Ya make me sick."

The dwarfs paid no attention to him. Doc scrubbed each of their bald heads with a brush. Bubbles floated all over the backyard.

"Heh, next thing ya know, she'll be tyin' your beards up in pink ribbons," Grumpy sneered. "She'll be smellin' ya up with that stuff called — uh — perfoom. Hah!"

The dwarfs had heard enough of Grumpy's remarks. They climbed out of the tub and formed a circle around him. "Get 'im!" shouted Doc. With that the dwarfs pounced on Grumpy and, with much slipping and sliding, managed to drag him over to the tub.

"Lemme go, ya fools!" Grumpy sputtered, but before he knew it, he was in the tub and being scrubbed clean.

"Ain't he sweet," laughed Bashful when Grumpy finally climbed out of the tub. "He smells like a petunia."

Snow White banged on the pot inside. "Food!" she called. The dwarfs went scurrying to the table ready to enjoy the meal.

"You'll pay dearly for this," muttered Grumpy, who trailed behind — but soon the smell of soup drew him into the cottage, as well.

8

To the dwarfs, supper that night was a feast beyond their wildest dreams. The soup was wonderful, and the pie filled them with delight.

Snow White felt as if she'd known the Seven Dwarfs all her life. They were so funny and sweet.

After the meal was finished, and the dishes cleaned and put away, the dwarfs decided it was time for a party. They were all fine yodelers, and they entertained Snow White by playing musical instruments and yodeling along with the music. Grumpy played his finely carved organ, Dopey beat a kettle drum, Sneezy and Bashful played concertinas, and Sleepy blew into a little horn shaped like a fish. Happy strummed a guitar-like instrument called a swanette. The music was lively and Snow White was soon tapping her foot and clapping along.

Doc walked up to Snow White and made a formal bow.

Snow White giggled and realized she was being asked to dance. Snow White took his hand, and soon

47

they were skipping around the room in time to the music.

Snow White hadn't had so much fun in many years. She had almost completely forgotten about her stepmother, the wicked Queen. Unfortunately the Queen had not forgotten about Snow White.

Back in the castle the Queen consulted her Magic Mirror. She was eager to hear it tell her that she was once again the fairest beauty in all the land. When the face in the Mirror appeared, she asked, "Who now is the fairest one of all?"

The face did not give her the answer she expected. "Over the seven jeweled hills, beyond the seventh fall," it said, "in the cottage of the Seven Dwarfs dwells Snow White — fairest one of all."

The Queen was confused. She held up the wooden box that the huntsman had handed her when he returned, pale and shaken, from the forest. In it was a small, red heart. The Queen opened the box and showed the heart to the face in the Mirror. "Snow White lies dead in the forest," she said. "The huntsman has brought me proof. Behold her heart."

"Snow White still lives," the Mirror revealed. " 'Tis the heart of a pig you hold in your hand."

"Then I've been tricked!" screamed the Queen.

The Queen slammed the lid of the box shut and stormed out of the chamber. "The heart of a pig," she muttered as she descended the castle steps. "The blundering fool!" The Queen went down, down,

into the most ancient chambers of the castle, until she reached her secret magical laboratory where she kept potions and books of magic spells.

A large black raven, the Queen's pet, flew above her head. It spread its wings wide and listened as the Queen raved in anger. "I'll go myself," she yelled, "to the dwarfs' cottage, in a disguise so complete no one will ever suspect." As she spoke the Queen looked over a shelf of dusty, ancient books. She pulled one down and began to read through it.

Finally she came to the secret spell she wanted. "Now, a formula to transform my beauty into ugliness — change my queenly gowns to a peddler's cloak."

The Queen was soon busy creating the potion she needed. "Mummy's dust to make me old," she muttered, sprinkling a pinch of gray powder into a glass. "To shroud my clothes — the black of night. To age my voice, an old hag's cackle." She poured more ingredients into the glass. "To whiten my hair, a scream of fright."

She took the glass and carried it over to a window. She shoved the window open and held up the glass. "A blast of wind to fan my hate," she cried. At her words a strong wind swept into the room. It blew out all the candles, throwing the room into total darkness. "A thunderbolt to mix it with," the wicked Queen continued, creating a jagged bolt of lightning in the sky.

"Now begin thy magic spell," she said, putting the potion to her blood-red lips. No sooner had she drunk than the Queen felt the room spinning around her. She clutched her throat. It felt as if it were on fire. Lightning flashed again in the sky, revealing that the potion's magic was indeed strong.

"Look! My hands!" said the Queen, seeing that her fingers were now crooked and bony. "My voice," she croaked, realizing that she now sounded like a very, very old woman. Lightning flashed again — the change was complete. The beautiful but evil Queen now looked as ugly on the outside as she was on the inside. Her hair was white, her nose was large and covered with warts. Her velvet gown was replaced by a dusty black cloak. "A perfect disguise," she laughed.

The Queen then opened another book of potions and paged through it. "And now," she cackled, "a special sort of death for one so fair. Hmmmmmm. What shall it be?"

"Ah!" she cried at last. She'd found a potion so cruel that it appealed to her evil nature. "A poison apple!"

The Queen clapped her hands together gleefully as she continued to read. "One taste of the poisoned apple, and the victim's eyes will close forever . . . in the sleeping death!"

9

While the Queen worked her terrible evil, unsuspecting Snow White continued to dance and sing with the dwarfs. Each of them was taking a turn in entertaining the others. When it was Bashful's turn to sing, he blushed from his forehead to his toes. "Oh, gosh," he giggled.

Grumpy gave Bashful a stern look and played the organ louder. "Oh, gosh," Bashful said again, brushing his soft brown shoes on the floor in front of him. Then, calling up all his courage, Bashful sang a little song.

When the song was over, Bashful suddenly felt shy again. He covered his face in his whiskers. The others laughed and picked up his song with their yodels. Snow White joined in, singing in harmony with the music.

When it came time for Dopey and Sneezy to perform, Dopey climbed onto Sneezy's shoulders and covered them with a long coat so that together they looked like one tall fellow. They asked Snow

White to dance, and all went well until Sneezy split them in two with a giant sneeze.

By the time the music stopped, Snow White had seen each of the dwarfs display a special musical talent. She fell back into one of the little chairs and laughed with delight.

"That was fun!" she said.

"Now you do somethin'," said Happy, not wanting the party to end.

"Well, what shall I do?" Snow White asked.

"Tell us a story," suggested Sleepy, who always loved a good bedtime story before going to sleep.

"Tell us a true story," Happy added.

"A loooove story," whispered Bashful shyly.

Snow White thought for a minute, then she folded her hands in her lap and began. "Well, once there was a princess. . . ."

"Was the princess — uh, you?" asked Doc.

Snow White just smiled at Doc and continued, "and she fell in love."

"Was it hard to do?" Sneezy asked.

"It was very easy," Snow White answered. "Anyone could see that the prince was charming — the only one for me."

The dwarfs liked this story. They leaned eagerly toward Snow White. "Was he — uh, strong and handsome?" asked Doc.

"Was he big and tall?" Sneezy wanted to know.

"There's nobody like him anywhere at all," Snow White told them.

She got a dreamy look on her face as she remembered the day she'd first seen the prince. She wondered if she would ever see him again. In her heart she somehow knew he would find her.

Suddenly the mechanical clock on the cottage wall chimed.

"Oh, my goodness!" said Snow White. She had been having such a good time she hadn't realized how late it was. "It's past bedtime. Go right upstairs to bed."

Remembering that they had to be up early to go to work, the dwarfs jumped up and began to climb the stairs. Doc caught Dopey by the tail of his long coat and called to the others. "Hold on there, men!"

They turned to look at him. "The princess will — a — sleep in our beds, upstairs," he told them.

"But where will you sleep?" asked Snow White.

"Oh, we'll be quite comfortable down here in a — a — in a — "

"In a pig's eye!" grumbled Grumpy, who did not want to give up his tiny bed.

"In a pig's sty — no, no, I mean," Doc went on, fumbling with the words, "I mean, we'll be comfortable, won't we, men?"

"Oh, yes," they answered, "mighty comfortable."

"Now don't you worry about us," said Doc, leading Snow White toward the stairs. Snow White looked at them doubtfully. "Are you sure?"

"Heh-heh! We'll be all right, ma'am," Happy spoke up.

"Go right on up now, — uh, my dear," said Doc, kindly.

"Well, if you insist," said Snow White, grateful for their kindness. "Good night."

"Good night, Princess," called the dwarfs.

"You're sure you'll be comfortable," Snow White asked half way up.the stairs.

"Oh, yes, very comfortable," they assured her.

Snow White wished them, "Pleasant dreams," and went up to bed. The minute she was gone the dwarfs dashed around the cottage looking for someplace to sleep. They tugged at pillows and argued over who would get to sleep in the drawers.

When they finally settled down, Sleepy was curled up in the woodpile, Doc was asleep in the sink, and Grumpy was muttering to himself as he tossed and turned trying to get comfortable inside the kettle. The others slept where they could, and soon the cottage was filled with the sound of snoring.

Upstairs Snow White said her prayers and asked

God to bless the dwarfs. She crawled into bed feeling safe and happy at last. But as she slept, the wicked Queen was working — working on a potion that would make Snow White sleep forever!

10

There would be no sleep for the wicked Queen that night. Now that she had changed herself into a horrible old witch, she was busy making a poison apple to give to Snow White.

"Dip the apple in the brew," she chanted as she dunked an apple tied to a string into a steaming kettle. "Let the sleeping death seep through."

When the Witch pulled the apple out of the brew she laughed at what she saw. A picture of a skull had formed on its skin. "The symbol of what lies within," she said. Then the Witch spoke these words over the apple: "Now turn red to tempt Snow White — to make her hunger for a bite." At this command, the skull disappeared, and the apple turned a deep, shiny red.

"Have a bite," the Witch said, holding the apple up to her pet raven. The black bird fluttered away fearfully causing the Witch to shriek with laughter. "It's not for you. It's for Snow White." The Witch rolled the apple in her bony hands. "When she breaks the tender peel to taste the apple in my hand, her breath will be still and her blood will thicken. Then I'll be the fairest in the land."

A disturbing thought then struck the Witch. "There may be an antidote — a cure for this poison." The Witch rushed to her book of spells and paged through it until she came to a section titled "Poison Apple Antidote." There was a cure! "The victim of the sleeping death can be awakened by love's first kiss," she read.

"No fear of that," she decided. "The dwarfs will think she's dead. She'll be buried alive."

Cackling to herself, the Witch filled a basket with apples and put the poison one on top. Then she lowered herself down through a trap door and descended the steps which led out of the castle and down to the river. A small boat awaited her there. The Witch climbed in and floated down-stream — away from the castle and into the forest.

The Witch let the river carry her into the darkest part of the forest. When she spotted some tall weeds, she paddled the boat into them and stepped out. Still clutching her basket of apples, the Witch made her way through the forest toward the cottage of the Seven Dwarfs.

Early the next morning, Snow White stood at the door of the cottage as the dwarfs prepared to go off to work. "Don't forget, my dear, the — the old Queen

is a sly one," Doc warned Snow White. "She's fulla witchcraft. So beware of strangers."

Snow White's heart was touched by his concern. "Don't worry," she said, lifting his cap and giving him a kiss on the forehead. "I'll be all right."

Doc didn't know what to do. He'd never been kissed before, but he liked it. "Eh — eh, yes — uh — wuh," he stammered. "Well, come on, men!"

"Be awful careful," said Bashful, " 'cause if anythin' should happen to you — I, ah — I, ah — "

Snow White smiled at the shy little dwarf. She bent down and kissed his head. "Good-bye," she said.

"Ooooh, gosh!" Bashful blushed and smiled.

"Heh! Disgustin'!" snorted Grumpy.

When it came Dopey's turn to be kissed, he lifted his face to Snow White. She planted a kiss on his bald head and said good-bye. Dopey twirled around in delight. He thought Snow White was just the most wonderful person in the world.

Snow White then kissed Sneezy, Happy, and Sleepy. When she looked up, there was Dopey again. He'd gotten to the back of the line and was waiting for another kiss. "Ha, ha, all right," laughed Snow White, planting another kiss on his head. "But that's the last."

Grumpy was the last to stomp out of the house. He marched past Snow White without a word, but then he turned back and said, "Now I'm warnin' ya.

Don't let nobody er nothin' in the house."

"Oh, Grumpy, you do care!" cried Snow White happily. Snow White kissed the scowling dwarf who broke away from her and ran. When Grumpy was sure no one could see him, he smiled and breathed a sigh of pleasure. Then he fixed his face into a frown and hurried to join the others.

As the dwarfs marched off, they never realized that they were passing right by the Witch, who was skulking through the woods toward the cottage. "The little men will be away, and she'll be alone," muttered the Witch, hearing the dwarfs' song in the distance. "Alone with a harmless old peddler woman."

As the Witch approached the cottage, she saw Snow White through the window. The animals were keeping her company as she rolled out the dough to top a pie. "Some day, my prince will come," she sang, still dreaming of the one she loved. The little birds made designs on the dough with their tiny feet and soon the pie was ready to bake.

Suddenly the shadow of the Witch fell across Snow White. She looked up, startled to see the old hag's face peering down at her through the open window.

"All alone, my pet?" the Witch asked.

"Why — why — yes, I am — but," Snow White answered, fearfully.

"The — the little men are not here?" the Witch continued.

"No, they're not."

"Hmmmmm," the Witch sniffed the baking pie, "makin' pies?"

"Yes, gooseberry pies," Snow White answered, telling herself not to be afraid of this poor old woman.

"It's apple pies that make the menfolks' mouths water," said the Witch, taking the poison apple from her basket, "pies made from apples like these."

The animals stared at the Witch, from the corner of the house. They had scurried away at the first sight of her. They knew there was something evil about this old woman.

Snow White reached through the window and took the poison apple from the Witch. "Oh, they do look delicious," she said.

"Yes," agreed the Witch, "but wait till you taste one, dearie."

Snow White's bird friends noticed something strange. Vultures sat in the trees around the cottage. Vultures were birds of death and did not usually live in the forest. They were a bad sign. Just as Snow White was about to take the poison apple, the little birds swooped from the trees and attacked the Witch, knocking the apple from her hand.

"Oh, oh, oh — go away!" cried the Witch, waving her arms in the air to frighten off the birds.

Snow White was horrified at the way the birds were acting. She didn't understand that they were trying to help her. She thought they were teasing a poor old woman. She ran to the front of the cottage

and shooed the birds away, shouting, "Stop it! Stop it! Go away!" The birds flew back to their branches. "Shame on you, frightening the poor old lady."

The Witch crawled on the ground looking for the poison apple, which had rolled away. She found it under a bush and quickly wiped it clean.

Snow White helped the Witch to her feet. "There, there, I'm sorry," she said comfortingly.

"Oh, my heart," gasped the Witch. "Oh my — my — poor heart. Take me into the house. Let me rest. A drink of water, please." Kind-hearted Snow White forgot all her fear and helped the old Witch into the house.

Once in the house, the Witch once again tried to get Snow White to taste the apple. "Because you've been so good to poor old Granny," she said, "I'll share a secret with you." The Witch picked up the poison apple and held it out to Snow White. "This is no ordinary apple. It's a Magic Wishing Apple."

"A Wishing Apple?" asked Snow White.

"Yes, one bite and all your dreams will come true."

"Really?" Snow White asked, already knowing what her dearest dream was — to find her prince.

"Yes, girlie," said the Witch, growing impatient. "Now make a wish . . . and take a bite."

The animals were watching all this from the window. They knew they had to go find the dwarfs and get them to return to the cottage. They ran off into the forest and caught up to the dwarfs just as they were about to enter the mine.

At first the dwarfs didn't know what to think. "What ails these crazy critters?" asked Doc.

"Yeah, they've gone — kow — kay — kwazy!" agreed Sneezy, sneezing from all the animal fur in the air.

The animals continued tugging at the dwarfs. "Go on, git outa here," Grumpy shooed the animals. But the animals wouldn't stop. They knew things were not well back at the cottage.

The animals were right. The Witch was just about to get Snow White to bite the apple. "Perhaps there's someone you love," coaxed the Witch.

"Well, there is someone," admitted Snow White.

"I thought so," cackled the Witch. "Old Granny knows a young girl's heart. Now take the apple, dearie — and make a wish."

"I wish," Snow White began.

As Snow White told the Witch of her wish, the animals kept trying to warn the dwarfs of the danger. Finally Grumpy got the message. "They ain't actin' this way for nothin'," he realized.

"Maybe the old Queen's got Snow White!" shouted Sleepy.

"The Queen!" cried Doc with alarm.

"The Queen will kill her!" said Grumpy. "We've gotta save her."

"Yes," agreed Doc, "but what'll we do?"

11

Grumpy jumped onto the back of one of the deer and motioned the other dwarfs to follow him. Soon the dwarfs and the animals were racing through the forest. The deer, each carrying one or two dwarfs, ran more swiftly than ever before. They leaped over logs and rocks. They knew there was not a moment to lose.

At the cottage, the Witch could barely conceal her impatience. She did not want to hear Snow White's wish. She just wanted her to bite the apple. "Fine, fine," she said sharply when Snow White finished telling her about the prince. "Now take a bite. Don't let the wish grow cold."

The moment finally came. Snow White put the apple to her lips and bit down on it. "Oh, I feel strange," she said at once.

"Her breath will grow still," chanted the Witch, "and her blood will thicken."

Snow White didn't understand. What was hap-

pening? She felt so dizzy. Suddenly she fell to the floor in a deep faint.

The Witch gazed down at the sleeping princess and screamed with laughter. "Now I'll be the fairest in the land!" she shrieked.

Just as she said this, the Witch heard the dwarfs dashing toward the cottage. She ran out the front door.

"There she goes!" cried Grumpy, who was the first to see her. The dwarfs and animals chased the Witch through the forest. The Witch managed to stay ahead of them as she hurried back toward the little boat she'd hidden near the river. Although she was ahead of them, every time the Witch turned around, the dwarfs were closer and closer.

Thunder cracked in the sky and rain poured down into the forest. In her panic, the Witch lost her way. Cries of "after her" and "there she is" filled her ears.

"Ohhhh!" screamed the furious Witch. "I'm trapped. What will I do?" She looked around and saw a rocky cliff. She thought she might be able to shake the dwarfs off her trail by climbing it. The dwarfs scampered up the rocks after her.

"I'll fix you," the Witch screamed back at them. "I'll fix you. I'll crush your bones." As she spoke, the Witch picked up the limb of a rotted tree and used it to pry a large boulder loose.

Grumpy was the first to see what the witch was doing. "Look out!" he warned the others. Just as the huge boulder was about to come tumbling down, a bolt of lightning hit the edge of the cliff where the Witch was standing. The ledge shattered, throwing the Witch over into the deep gorge below. The huge boulder fell after her.

The dwarfs reached the edge of the cliff and looked over. There below them was the dead body of the Witch. She was surrounded by the vultures who had followed her into the forest.

The dwarfs hurried back to their cottage as fast as they could. They dashed into the front room only to find Snow White on the floor, the poison apple still in her soft hands.

Grumpy was the first to break into a loud sob. "We're too late," he wailed, "too late." In minutes the other dwarfs began to cry, and the cottage was filled with the sound of weeping.

Assuming that Snow White was dead, the dwarfs lit candles and held a vigil for the tender-hearted princess whom they had come to love so dearly.

12

Snow White was so beautiful, even in death, that the dwarfs could not find it in their hearts to bury her. They built a coffin of glass and gold, and they kept watch over Snow White day and night.

The prince, who had been searching everywhere for Snow White, heard of a maiden who lay dead in a glass coffin. Hoping this was not his beloved, he set out into the forest to see for himself.

He soon came to the cottage of the Seven Dwarfs. When he saw Snow White lying so still in her coffin, he was overwhelmed with sadness. He stood on the edge of the forest singing the love song he'd first sung to Snow White on the day they met. As he sang, he saw the dwarfs come from the cottage and place fresh flowers around Snow White's coffin. He watched as they rolled back the glass cover of the coffin so that they could gaze upon her fair face once again.

The prince, too, longed to see Snow White one last time. He walked slowly up to the coffin. When

the dwarfs saw the sorrow in his eyes, they knew at once that he was the prince Snow White had longed for.

The prince knelt by her side and gently kissed Snow White. Then he bowed his head and knelt in silent prayer next to the dwarfs. Even the forest animals stood still, with bowed heads to show their love for Snow White.

Then, very, very slowly at first, Snow White began to move. Love's first kiss had overcome the sleeping death!

The prince and the dwarfs watched, awestruck, as Snow White sat up and looked around. When Snow White saw the prince, she reached out to him. He quickly swept Snow White up in his arms.

The dwarfs yelled with joy. Doc and Grumpy hugged one another. Happy and Sneezy threw their hats in the air. The animals leaped around Snow White and the prince.

Snow White kissed each of the dwarfs joyfully. Then the prince carried her to his horse, and, still waving good-bye to the dwarfs, Snow White let him lead her out of the forest and home to his castle where . . . they lived happily ever after.

THE END

74

The Making of
Walt Disney's Movie
Snow White
and the Seven Dwarfs

In 1934 Walt Disney had a bold new idea. He wanted to make a full-length animated movie using the beloved fairytale *Snow White and the Seven Dwarfs*. Everyone told him he was crazy. Up until then, no one had seen a cartoon movie before. The only cartoons were short ones that were shown before live-action movies. People told Walt that audiences wouldn't spend money for a ticket to see a movie that had no big movie stars in it.

Walt Disney was so sure that people would like *Snow White* that he spent all the money he'd made on his popular short cartoons, and then borrowed another quarter of a million dollars. He spent one and a half million dollars (which was quite a lot in the lean years of America's Depression) to hire 750 artists who worked for three years on *Snow White*.

Why did *Snow White* take so long? Walt wanted to make sure everything was perfect. For example, each of the dwarfs has an entirely different walk. Having them walk in a line, each with his different walk, took four artists six months of work — even though the scene in which they come home singing "Hi-ho" is only about three minutes long!

Creating the character of Snow White was even more painstaking. A real actress named Marge Champion acted out the entire movie before film cameras. The Disney artists then traced her movements from the film and redrew her as a cartoon character.

Snow White and the Seven Dwarfs opened in a Los Angeles theater on December 21, 1937. Walt Disney had been right. People loved his movie. They loved it so much that in 1939 it won a special Academy Award. Shirley Temple presented Walt Disney with one big Oscar statue — and seven tiny ones!